Hopple Hare
A hare with a nose for mystery
and a heart for friendship

Copyright © 2001 by Michael Neugebauer Verlag, an
imprint of Nord-Süd Verlag AG, Gossau Zürich, Switzerland
First published in Switzerland under the title *Das Gelbe Ding*
English translation copyright © 2002 by North-South Books Inc., New York

First published in the United States, Great Britain, Canada,
Australia, and New Zealand in 2002 by North-South Books,
an imprint of Nord-Süd Verlag AG, Gossau Zürich, Switzerland.

Distributed in the United States by North-South Books Inc., New York.

Library of Congress Cataloging-in-Publication Data is available.
A CIP catalogue record for this book is available from The British Library.
ISBN 0-7358-1593-3 (trade edition) 10 9 8 7 6 HC 5 4 3 2 1
ISBN 0-7358-1594-1 (library edition) 10 9 8 7 6 LE 5 4 3 2 1
Printed in Italy

For more information about our books, and the authors and artists
who create them, visit our web site: www.northsouth.com

THE GREAT GOLDEN THING

By Linard Bardill
Illustrated by Miriam Monnier
Translated by J. Alison James

A Michael Neugebauer Book

North-South Books
New York / London

Once there was a little country nestled
between an oak forest and high snowy
mountains. To the north was
a small lake, with an island.
Flowing from this lake were
a rushing river and a
meandering stream.
Both brook and river
met again at the South Sea. Bramble Bear
and his mate, Brindle Bear, lived
in a cave at the edge of the woods.
Hopple Hare gardened next to the stream.
And Gimli, the magician, lived in a little hut
on a hill, right in the middle of the land.

Behind Gimli's home, a spring of pure water
burst out of the rocks, flowed into a small pool, and
trickled back into the ground again. Everyone was welcome
to this water, but it was Gimli who took care of it and thanked it
with blossoms when the trees were in bloom.

"You quench my thirst, cool my brow, and nourish my fruit
trees," Gimli said to the spring every day. "The least
I can do for you is offer you fresh flowers,
for I know you love them so."

The spring looked forward to the flowers
Gimli promised, but the flowers seldom
came, for once the blossoms on Gimli's
trees were gone, there were no more
flowers on his hill, none in all the
land. There was fruit, and
mushrooms, carrots, and
even grass. But the
spring liked flowers.

One afternoon, when Gimli was watering his trees,
he heard a deep voice call out his name.
Then Bramble Bear came around the corner.
"What is it, Bramble Bear?" asked Gimli.
"I saw something!" Bramble Bear was out of breath.
"Something huge! Something gold! A great golden thing!"
"I see," said Gimli, who didn't. "A great golden thing?"

Bramble Bear sat down to catch his breath. "I have never seen such a thing," he said. "It was so big, it was frightening."

"Ah," said Gimli wisely. "And just how big was this thing?"

"This big," said Bramble Bear, holding out his paws as wide as a soup bowl. "Or maybe it was this big. No, a little smaller. Or maybe . . . yes, I'm sure, it was exactly this size."

Bramble Bear looked frightened. "Do you think it is dangerous?"

Gimli scratched his beard. "It could be dangerous, if it is as big as you say, only … I must know more. Did you notice anything else?"

Bramble Bear pondered this awhile before he said, "I saw some green. Yes, it had green as well, but not much."

"So," said Gimli thoughtfully. "This great golden thing, with some green, did it fly do you think? Or was it on the ground?"

Bramble Bear wrinkled his forehead and said, "That is a difficult question. It was on the ground and yet it flew as well. The green was like a leg that stood on the ground but the gold, which rested on top of the green, flew in the air. Do you think it might sting?"

"Golden things that fly in the air often sting," said Gimli. "But I've never heard of one quite so large. I think you need to take me there so I can see for myself, for I cannot imagine what it could be."

So the two of them went down the hill to investigate
what this mysterious great golden thing could be.
When they got to the stream near the woods,
they met Hopple Hare.

"Where are you going, with your foreheads
  wrinkled and your footsteps rushed?"
  asked Hopple Hare.
  Bramble Bear greeted his friend.
"We are on an investigation," he explained,
"to discover the identity of a great golden thing
  that flies, yet rests on a leg that's green and
  stands on the ground."
"It sounds dangerous," said Hopple Hare.
"But Gimli is with us," said Bramble Bear.
"Then I shall come, too," announced
  Hopple Hare.

Bramble Bear's mate, Brindle Bear, poked her nose out of her cave
as they walked past.
"What are you three up to?" she asked suspiciously.
Hopple Hare said,"We are on an investigation to discover the identity of a great
golden thing that flies, yet rests on a leg that's green and stands on the ground."
"What was that?" asked Brindle Bear."Something gold? Something large?"
"Yes, yes," said Hopple Hare worriedly."And it flies. But it rests on a leg . . ."
"That is green," interrupted Brindle Bear.
Bramble Bear nodded. "Even Gimli doesn't know what to make of it," he said.

Brindle Bear smiled widely. "Could you possibly be talking about my sunflower?" she said. "I planted a sunflower at the edge of the woods. Every day I have given it a bucket of the special spring water from behind Gimli's house. Now it has grown wonderfully big."

"A sunflower?" they all said at once, knowing she must be right.
"Oh," said Hopple Hare sadly. "Our investigation is over before it's begun.
And I was so looking forward to the discovery."
"I am very embarrassed," said Bramble Bear. "I thought it was dangerous."
They couldn't bear the disappointment.

Brindle Bear laughed again. "Just because you know what it is doesn't mean you can't look for it," she said.

"Absolutely right," said Gimli, and the three friends hurried down to the woods.

There they saw the sunflower. And it *was* a great golden thing! It stood as high as Gimli's hut. The golden petals flickered in the soft wind. It swayed gently on a green stalk, as elegant as a flower could be. They stared in wonder.

"You know," said Hopple Hare. "If Bramble Bear hadn't been so curious, we might never have seen this magnificent flower."

They sang songs and danced beneath the flower. And the flower fluttered her petals as if she wanted to take leave of her green leg and fly off above them.

Gimli gathered the petals that had fallen to the ground. They were still fresh and lovely. He laid them gently in his bag to take back to his spring. "For the spring really does love flowers," he explained to his friends.